NINJA MEERKATS

Read all the Ninja Meerkats adventures!

The Clan of the Scorpion (#1)

The Eye of the Monkey (#2)

Escape from Ice Mountain (#3)

Hollywood Showdown (#4)

The Tomb of Doom (#5)

Big City Bust-Up (#6)

The Ultimate Dragon Warrior (#7)
available Winter 2014

Outback Attack (#8)
available Winter 2014

BIG CITY BUST-UP

GARETH P. JONES

SQUARE FISH
NEW YORK

SQUARE
FISH

An Imprint of Macmillan
175 Fifth Avenue
New York, NY 10010
mackids.com

NINJA MEERKATS: BIG CITY BUST-UP.

Square Fish books may be purchased for business or promotional use.
For information on bulk purchases, please contact the Macmillan Corporate
and Premium Sales Department at (800) 221-7945 x5442
or by e-mail at specialmarkets@macmillan.com.

Library of Congress Cataloging-in-Publication Data Available
ISBN 978-1-250-03403-8 (paperback) / ISBN 978-1-250-04599-7 (e-book)

Originally published in Great Britain by Stripes Publishing
First Square Fish Edition: 2013
Square Fish logo designed by Filomena Tuosto

10 9 8 7 6 5 4 3 2 1

For Ella and Billy Brimble

~ G P J

Oh, hello there. I trust you've been well. I'm afraid I've been rather under the weather myself. Although how one can be anything *other* than under the weather, I don't know. You can't exactly be *over* the weather, can you? I went to see my doctor this morning and he asked what the problem was.

"I can only turn left," I said. "Everything I do, it's always left."

He gave me a tablet to take and said I would be all right in the morning. But that won't be much better, will it? I'll still be going around in circles.

Thankfully, the Clan of the Scorpion know how to go straight to where the action is. They are four young meerkats in the prime of their lives, forever ready to use their ninja skills to battle against the forces of evil.

Jet Flashfeet: a super-fast ninja whose only fault is craving the glory he so richly deserves.

Bruce "the muscle" Willowhammer: the strongest of the gang, though in the brain race he lags somewhat behind.

Donnie Dragonjab: a brilliant mind, inventor, and master of gadgets.

Chuck Cobracrusher: his clear leadership has saved the others' skins more times than I care to remember.

Oh, and me, Grandmaster One-Eye: as old and wise as the sand dunes themselves.

This story is about the time I sent them to London on a secret mission. I would have gone myself, but I was feeling rather unwell then, too. When you get to my age, it's to be expected. So I'll finish with a poem by another sickly old meerkat by the name of Milo Erback-Hurtz.

There was a time when I
Jumped so high in the sky,
I could throw a pie
And hit a crow in the eye.
Now when I try,
The only eye I can hit with the pie
Would be a wingless fly
That was crawling by.

Anyway, on with the story of . . .
BIG CITY BUST-UP.

LONDON CALLING

In the early evening hustle and bustle of Covent Garden no one paid any attention to the automatic street-cleaning machine that trundled over the cobbles, whisking up discarded trash with its two spinning brushes. Certainly, no one suspected that inside the machine were four Ninja Meerkats.

Donnie was sitting at the front, using a control that he had installed to override the automatic route of the cleaner. He steered the machine around the tourists, market stalls, and street performers that filled the famous London square. Jet, Chuck, and Bruce were behind him, squeezed around a long tube that ran through the middle of the cabin, which sucked up trash into a large container at the back of the vehicle.

"This is an excellent disguise, Donnie," said Chuck.

"Actually it's a *rubbish* disguise," said Jet, with a chuckle.

Bruce pulled his head out of a take-out box and said, "Rubbish? It's the first one we've used that actually collects food—it's brilliant."

"I can't believe you're eating again," said Jet. "You ate twelve bags of jellied crickets on the plane here."

"That was just a snack. Look, I found half a burger," Bruce exclaimed, excitedly holding up the soggy specimen. He took a big bite. "Hmm, there's a bit too much ketchup, but it's nice of them to leave the pickle in."

"Bruce, you don't know where that's been," said Chuck, wrinkling his nose in disgust.

"Yeah, but I know where it's going," he replied, taking another huge bite.

Donnie pressed a button and the machine came to a standstill. "The meeting point is directly below us," he said. He pressed another button, which opened a hatch in the base of the vehicle, revealing a drain below. "This must be the way in."

"I wonder why Grandmaster One-Eye told us to come here. It's all very mysterious," said Jet.

"He said he received a message from an old friend," said Chuck. "And that it was a top secret mission."

"Hey, look! Street entertainers," said Bruce, distracted by a man juggling with flaming torches next to the vehicle.

"Fire juggling. Pah!" said Jet. "If I was a street performer I'd demonstrate my new move, the Quake Maker."

"What's that?" asked Bruce.

"I'll show you."

"Jet, no!" started Donnie. "Not inside the—"

It was too late. Jet leaped up and came crashing back down. Had they been outside, the force would have caused the ground to shake, knocking anyone nearby off their feet. But inside the street cleaner it had a different effect—the entire vehicle collapsed in a heap.

"Whoops! Sorry," said Jet.

"Bruce, Jet, Donnie," yelled Chuck. "Into the drain before anyone spots us!"

Donnie keyed a code into a tiny keypad on the drain cover and it slid open. One by one, each of the meerkats slipped through, sliding down a chute and dropping into the pitch-black drain below.

"Where are we?" asked Bruce. "I can't see a thing."

There was an electronic whirring as the drain cover slid back over the entry point. A light flickered on to reveal that they were in a room filled with technological gadgetry. The walls were lined with screens displaying CCTV footage from all around London. Sitting by a console covered in rows of buttons was a lumbering bulldog wearing a small bowler hat. He turned to face them, revealing that he had a monocle in his left eye and a scar down the right side of his face.

"Quite an entrance," he said. "It reminds me of the time I had to evacuate a tank after some fool pulled the pin out of a grenade, thinking he was opening a tin of sardines." He chuckled. "Clan of the Scorpion, thank you for responding to my request for assistance. Allow me to introduce myself. I'm Major Works, chief of the British Secret Secret Service."

"The Secret Service?" said Donnie.

"No-no-no," said the major, shaking his head so that his jowls flapped about. "Every Tom, Dick, and Harry knows about the Secret Service. This is the *Secret* Secret Service."

"What's the difference?" asked Bruce.

"The Secret Secret Service is actually a secret."

"And you need our help?" asked Chuck.

"Yes, well," said the major, adjusting his monocle. "We don't normally recruit outsiders, but all my spies have gone missing. It's a very peculiar business."

"Missing?" said Jet.

"Yes, I'm afraid so. I have operatives all over the place. There's a spaniel in Spain, an Afghan in Argentina, a Pekinese in Paris . . . Not to mention all the others. But they've all disappeared and we don't know who's behind it. This mission is of highest national importance so I contacted old One-Eye, hoping he might be able to help, and he recommended you."

"How do you know Grandmaster One-Eye?" asked Donnie.

"Agent One-Eye has been of great assistance to the Secret Secret Service in the past," replied the bulldog.

"He was a spy?" exclaimed Jet. "That's so cool."

"He once prevented an attack on London by the Seventeen Samurai Sheep of Shetland—specialists in sabotage, don't you know. Agent One-Eye secreted himself in a shepherd's bag, infiltrated the flock, and fed us information to stop them."

"So he was a shepherd spy?" said Donnie, chuckling. "Shepherd's pie? Get it?"

"No," said Bruce.

"And if he had been hiding in a cottage, he'd have been a cottage spy," added Jet.

Major Works looked confused.

"Major Works," said Chuck seriously, "please tell us what our mission is. While our enemy the Ringmaster is lying low, we are ready to assist you."

The major pressed a button and a glass cabinet appeared on one of the screens. It was filled with expensive-looking gold items encrusted with sparkling jewels. "These are the crown jewels," he said. "They are kept underground at the Tower of London and guarded by the country's top security. Three days ago someone entered the Tower undetected and made off with the royal orb."

"What's the royal orb?" asked Jet.

Major Works pointed to a golden globe with a cross on the top.

"Nothing else was taken?" asked Donnie.

"No. Just the orb."

"How did they get around the security?" asked Chuck.

"The guards in the Jewel House were all rendered unconscious by some kind of knock-out gas that came in through the vents," said the major.

"What about the CCTV?" asked Donnie. "You seem to have the whole city covered."

"There are a few blind spots, I'll admit, but you're right—the coverage is pretty good and there *is* a camera in the Jewel House of the Tower." The major clicked another button and some of the screens showed different views of the Tower of London, including one overlooking the jewels themselves. "This is how everything looked before the robbery," he explained. "Now watch carefully." Slowly the picture fizzled away until all the screens were completely blank.

"They've been scrambled," said Donnie. "Didn't anyone notice this happen?"

"The security guards watching the live surveillance footage were also knocked out. No one knew anything was amiss until the guards woke up and found the orb gone."

The major pressed a button and the images returned to the screens.

"Maybe it was those birds," suggested Bruce, pointing out a number of large black birds in the grounds of the Tower.

"No-no-no," replied the major, once again wobbling his jowls. "Those are the ravens that live in the Tower. They're so doddery, they don't know what's going on. Legend has it that if they ever leave, the Tower will fall to the ground. But they're so old they couldn't go anywhere if they tried."

"Is there any reason why someone would target the orb? Will the thief try to sell it?" asked Donnie.

The major shifted uncomfortably. "Well . . . never mind that . . . But it's imperative that it is returned as soon as possible."

"Why? What's so important about it?" asked Chuck.

"I'm afraid I can say no more. Unlike the Secret Service, *we* pride ourselves on secrecy here at the Secret Secret Service. Now, will you help?"

"Yes," said Chuck, bowing graciously. "We will find your orb. You have my word. Donnie, any ideas?"

"I should be able to descramble the footage," he replied.

"Is that possible?" asked the major.

"Oh, yes. It'll take me a couple of hours with someone to help me," said Donnie. "But I can definitely do it."

"Good," said Chuck. "Bruce, stay here and help Donnie. Jet and I will go to the Tower and see what we can find out."

"I'd be grateful if you could wear these," said Major Works, handing Jet what looked like an ordinary pair of sunglasses. "They have a camera on the front and a microphone and speakers on the sides. That way I can see what you're doing and communicate with you at all times."

"Why me?" asked Jet.

"Oh, if you don't want to, perhaps Mr. Cobracrusher will," said Major Works. "I need to be in constant communication with our top agent, but since you're all new to this . . ."

"I'll wear them," said Jet quickly, putting on the sunglasses.

"Excellent work, Agent Flashfeet. We'll make a secret secret agent out of you yet."

"Fine," said Chuck. "Now, Donnie—Jet and I will need a disguise."

"I have just the thing," replied Donnie.

CHAPTER TWO

A TRIP TO THE TOWER

The major led the meerkats out of the control room and up some steps. A panel in the wall slid open and they stepped out into a quiet courtyard just off Covent Garden.

"Agent Flashfeet, Agent Cobracrusher, good luck on your mission," said Major Works. "Agent Willowhammer and Agent Dragonjab, I'll see you back in the control room."

He went back inside and Donnie pulled out what looked like a flattened gray bird. "It's my new disguise, complete with working wings," he said, carefully unfolding it. "I call it the Carrier Pigeon."

"And it actually flies?" asked Chuck, looking at it doubtfully. "I mean, it's been tried and tested, hasn't it?"

"Of course! Well . . . I *tried* to test it. It did crash, but only a little bit and I've improved it since then."

"OK," said Chuck. "Jet–"

"You mean Agent Flashfeet," said Jet.

"OK. Agent Flashfeet, climb in. Bruce, can you help him?"

While Bruce helped Jet into the costume, Chuck took Donnie to one side, away from Jet and his sunglasses. "There's something Major Works isn't telling us," he said. "We must try to discover what it is."

"Agreed," said Donnie.

"Also, I fear Jet is a little taken with playing spy."

They could hear Jet humming the tune to one of his favorite spy movies.

“You think?!” said Donnie.

They turned to see Jet inside the bird disguise, peering out of the beady glass eyes.

“Where’s mine?” asked Chuck.

“I should have mentioned that the Carrier Pigeon is only really designed for one,” said Donnie.

“Don’t worry, I’ll get you in,” said Bruce.

“Really?” said Chuck uncertainly.

“Oh, yeah,” said Bruce. He grabbed Chuck and thrust him into the rear half of the bird disguise. “It’s like Christmas–stuffing a bird.”

“Ouch,” yelped Jet.

“Sorry, that was my sword,” said Chuck’s muffled voice.

“Hold on, I’ll zip you up,” said Bruce,

tucking Chuck's tail in to avoid getting his fur caught in the zipper. Once he had finished it looked more like a feathery sack of potatoes than a bird.

"It's quite a tight fit," said Chuck.

"Hey, Chuck, it tickles when you talk," said Jet.

"Jet, can you see the row of buttons in front of you?" said Donnie.

"Yep," replied Jet.

"Press the one marked 'stand.'"

Jet did so and the bird's legs suddenly stood bolt upright.

"Now press the one that says 'walk,'" said Donnie.

Jet pressed the button and the bird began walking forward, making an electronic clicking noise as it moved.

"There's a joystick for controlling direction," said Donnie.

Jet turned the bird around.

"To make it fly you need to get a bit of speed up, then press the button marked 'fly,'" said Donnie.

Jet pushed the joystick forward and the bird began to run.

"Wait!" said Donnie. "I haven't told you how to land."

But Jet and Chuck couldn't hear him above the clicking noise.

Jet pressed the "fly" button and the wings began to flap. Gradually the bird took to the air, soaring up and narrowly avoiding a brick wall.

"Ninja-zoom!" shouted Jet. "Agent Flashfeet is in the air."

"Something tells me I should be grateful that I can't see anything," said Chuck.

"Don't worry, you're in safe hands, Chuck. I was born to fly—that's why Mom called me Jet." He laughed. "Now, which way are we going?"

At that moment, Major Works's voice crackled through Jet's sunglasses. "The

Tower is east of here. You see that river down there? That's the Thames. Follow it to the left. The Tower isn't far."

In the back, Chuck wasn't feeling at all well, especially since Jet insisted on catching rising air currents and performing bold loop-the-loops for fun. He was relieved when Jet finally announced that he could see the Tower.

"Donnie didn't tell us how to land!" shouted Chuck. "Contact Major Works through the headset, Jet! Donnie should be with him, unscrambling the footage."

"You worry too much," said Jet, gliding to the right. "I've got the hang of this thing now. Hold on tight."

Chuck felt the bird fall into a nosedive and heard Jet whoop with excitement.

"Jet . . . I really think you should check with Donnie before landing," he said.

"Nah," said Jet. "Landing's just like taking off but the other way around. Brace yourself!"

"Je-et!" yelled Chuck, as they went swooping down inside the grounds of the Tower, brushing their wings on one of the turrets and zooming over the head of a guard. As Jet brought the bird in to land, its legs hit the ground and snapped clean off, sending it bumping along the ground.

"See, I told you I could land it," said Jet, as the bird finally came to a standstill.

"I think we should swap places," groaned Chuck.

"Not now, we've got company," said Jet.

Two large black ravens ambled over to look at the strange pigeon that had just crash-landed.

“Oh, it’s a pigeon,” said one. “I say, old bird, one can’t land in here, you know.”

The other bird looked at him with a puzzled expression. “You can’t stand it here, Jonnie? Well, why do you stay?”

“*Land* in here, Larry,” shouted the first. “I’m telling this pigeon he can’t fly in here.”

“Yes, it can be, can’t it?” said Larry, nodding.

"Can be what?"

"Flying can be rather dear, can't it?"

"No, no, no," said Jonnie, raising his voice. "I'm talking about him flying . . . FLYING!" he yelled. "USING YOUR WINGS."

"I'm losing my wings?" said the other, looking to check they were still there.

"Not losing. Using . . ." bellowed Jonnie. "U-SING!"

"Oh, if you like." Larry began to sing. "God save our gracious Queen . . ."

"We're here about the missing orb," shouted Jet. "DO YOU KNOW ANYTHING ABOUT THE MISSING ORB?"

"There's no need to shout, old bird. *He's* the deaf one," replied Jonnie. "Yes, that was a terrible business. No one saw a thing, you know."

"You didn't see anything suspicious at all?" asked Jet.

"See any fishes?" said Larry, who had stopped singing.

"Larry, leave this to me," said Jonnie. "No, we have no idea who took the orb."

"Oh, *the orb,*" said Larry. "Of course, it's what's kept *inside* that really matters."

"Hush, Larry. We're not to speak about that," scolded Jonnie.

"What *is* kept inside?" asked Jet.

"You had better leave now," said Jonnie abruptly. "We can't help. And if one of the guards spots a pigeon in here, you'll be in trouble!"

The two ravens turned and walked away, talking to each other as they went.

"I couldn't hear a word he was saying," said Larry.

"That's pigeon English for you," replied Jonnie.

"We should go," said Chuck, "before we

draw too much attention to ourselves."

"How are we going to take off with no legs?" said Jet.

"This situation calls for me to make a stand," said Chuck. He kicked his legs through the bottom of the disguise and stood up. The odd-shaped pigeon looked even odder with two furry meerkat legs poking out. Chuck started running as fast as he could.

"That's it," said Jet. "Keep up the speed." He pressed the button marked "fly" and the wings began to flap, sending the bird soaring up into the sky.

"And please fly more sedately this time!" said Chuck.

"What does sedately mean?" asked Jet.

"It means no more loop-the-loooooo—"

Chuck's words were lost as Jet executed a spectacular loop-the-loop over Tower Bridge.

CHAPTER THREE

PANIC ON THE STREETS OF LONDON

The sun was setting over London as Jet brought the pigeon disguise down in the quiet courtyard off Covent Garden. He gave Chuck just enough warning of when his feet would touch the ground and they managed a clumsy landing. They both squeezed out of the disguise and, as they approached the entrance to the headquarters, the panel slid open automatically. Downstairs, in the control room, they found Donnie frantically pressing buttons and pulling levers on the console, while Bruce lay underneath it,

following Donnie's instructions. Major Works was monitoring the screens.

"Bruce, connect the red and the blue wires," shouted Donnie.

"OK," said Bruce.

"How are you doing, Donnie?" asked Chuck.

"We're almost there," replied Donnie.

"What did you find out?"

"Not much," said Jet, "except that those ravens are stark *raven* mad."

"I did warn you," said the major, without turning around.

"Major Works," said Chuck. "One of the ravens mentioned that there is something inside the orb."

The major coughed and said, "Yes, well—"

"Ah-ha!" exclaimed Donnie, interrupting him. "Got it. Bruce, disconnect the blue wire and reattach the yellow. Major, would you mind bringing up the footage again?"

Major Works tapped a couple of buttons and several screens showed different views of the Tower of London. "Crystallized conkers!" he exclaimed. "It's the missing footage."

"I knew it," said Donnie. "They depixelated the network while recoding the system override using a roaming code, making it nearly impossible to unscramble. It looks like there is some kind of localized scrambler."

"What's that in English?" asked the major.

"Whoever did this knows what they're doing," said Donnie. "Look carefully at the picture on this screen and you should be able to see a small flashing light. That's the device that is sending out the scrambling signal."

"There," said Chuck. "On that statue."

Chuck pointed out a statue of a knight in the corner with a flashing light coming from it. They watched as gas spilled out of the air vents and the guards collapsed to the ground.

"Now the thief will reveal himself," said the major.

They kept their eyes on the door, expecting it to open, but the thief was already in the room. What they had taken to be a statue was actually a man, standing still and disguised as a knight. He walked up to the cabinet containing the jewels, cut a hole in the glass, and removed the orb.

"His helmet must double up as a gas mask," said Donnie. "This guy is good."

"Rollicking radishes!" exclaimed the major. "It must be the Human Statue."

"You know this man?" asked Chuck.

"Yes." Major Works typed something into the console and brought up various images of a man dressed in different statue disguises. Data about his previous crimes scrolled down the side of the screen. "Real name, Stan Still," said Major Works. "Known as the Human Statue, he is a former street performer with a grudge against the world. Fed up with being ignored by a public that doesn't appreciate his skills, he began using his talents for causing havoc. He is a professional thief, an electronics expert, and a pickpocket. He's also a parkour master."

"What? A master of parking cars?" said Bruce.

"*Parkour* not parker," blustered the major. "Free running, the skill of jumping from rooftop to rooftop. I should have guessed he would be behind this. He escaped from prison several months ago."

On the screen, the knight marched out of the room carrying the orb.

Jet said, "So we just need to find this Human Statue character and recover the orb. Simple."

"Ye-es," said Major Works doubtfully.

"Major, if there's anything else you should tell us, now's the time," said Chuck.

"Um, well . . ." A red light on the console started to flash. "I'd better check what this is," he said.

He hit a couple of buttons and an image of Piccadilly Circus appeared. The major's look quickly turned to horror when he saw what was happening at the busy tourist spot.

The footage didn't have sound, but if it had, it would have been the sound of screaming. The winged statue that sat at the top of the fountain had come to life, and terrified people were running everywhere. He was hovering over his pedestal and firing arrows at anyone who came near.

"Blistering bunions!" exclaimed the major. "He's using it already!"

"Using what?" demanded Chuck.

Before he could explain, the Human Statue appeared on the screen. He was no longer dressed as a knight but wore a flat cap. He slipped through the crowds toward a statue of four horses and tapped them.

Seconds later, the horses sprang to life. They leaped forward and galloped down the street. People ran to get out of their way as they thundered past.

"We have to stop him," said Chuck. "Clan of the Scorpion, let's go!"

There was no time for clever disguises, so the meerkats relied on their speed and stealth training to avoid being seen as they made their way through the streets.

As they turned the corner into Trafalgar Square they were confronted by a scene of utter chaos. The winged archer had been joined by the four horses, plus another horse with a regal-looking gentleman on its back, and a man with a bowler hat and long bendy cane.

Sirens could be heard everywhere as riot police piled out of vans and surrounded the square. They rushed forward, clutching their riot shields, but a man and a dolphin were keeping them at bay by firing jets of water from a fountain.

"Follow me," urged Chuck, leading the

others behind the line of police, along a wall, and then up onto an empty plinth. From there they could see that the Human Statue was standing in front of one of the oversized lions at the base of Nelson's Column. He touched the lion's nose and it instantly came to life, stood up, and prowled around the column. The Human Statue did the same to another lion, then began to scale the column with astonishing agility. He was heading toward the statue of Lord Nelson.

"Major Works," said Chuck, addressing the camera on Jet's sunglasses. "How is he doing this?"

"There's no time for that!" replied the major. "You need to bring the fellow in. That's King George the Fourth on the horse, and the chap with the stick is Charlie Chaplin. Stop him before he gets Nelson too!"

"Right. Let's go," said Jet, making a dash for the column.

"We need a proper pla—" began Chuck.

But it was too late. The statues had spotted Jet. George the Fourth drew his sword and charged. Jet dodged the attack and landed a powerful double-fist punch on the horse's head. It staggered back, but quickly rallied.

"Wow," said Jet, shaking his hand. "It's like punching a rock."

"Funny that," said Donnie.

The king swung his sword again and Jet jumped over it in the nick of time, then spun around and kicked the horse's legs. It barely registered his attack.

"Donnie," said Chuck. "Bruce and I will keep the others busy. You and Jet concentrate on getting the Human Statue down."

"OK," said Donnie.

"Time for some Bruce Force!" cried Bruce, rolling forward, then springing up into the face of a huge lion and placing an almighty punch between its eyes. The blow would have knocked out an elephant, but it had little effect on the bronze lion.

Donnie opened his bag and pulled out a grappling hook. Suddenly he heard a THWACK come down beside him and looked up to see the statue of Charlie Chaplin using his cane as a weapon. The statue went to strike again, but this time the cane was blocked by Chuck's sword. Had it been a normal stick, Chuck's mighty blade would have cut straight through it, but it did nothing more than CLANK loudly against it. The sword fight that ensued bought Donnie enough time to fire the grappling hook at the Human Statue.

The hook wrapped around the Human Statue's feet just as he grabbed the top of the column. Donnie yanked it, but the villain held on tightly. He gave it another tug, but the Human Statue fought back, reached up, and managed to touch the ankle of Lord Nelson. Instantly Nelson came to life, reached down, and sliced through Donnie's line with his sword, freeing the Human Statue, who pulled himself onto the top of the column.

Below, the police had fought their way into the square itself.

"Agent Flashfeet," Jet heard Major Works say through the speaker on his sunglasses. "As agents of the Secret Secret Service, you must remain unseen. Find a hiding spot for you and your colleagues. The police should be able to handle the situation from here."

"What? Give up?" exclaimed Jet.

"The police have the place surrounded

and the Human Statue is stuck at the top of the column. I need you to get your team out of sight, Agent Flashfeet."

"My team. I like the sound of that," said Jet. "Yes, sir."

"Donnie," Jet said, "we've been ordered to take cover."

"Since when do you take orders?" asked Donnie.

"Since I became a secret secret agent," said Jet. "You get Chuck. I'll get Bruce and meet you in that bin over there."

"Yes, sir, Agent Flashfeet," replied Donnie, with a cheeky wink.

Inside the bin, the meerkats had a good view of the top of the column, where the Human Statue was standing beside Lord Nelson.

"What's he doing?" asked Bruce. "He's got nowhere to go."

Suddenly, the Human Statue bent down and touched the top of the column, making it bend like rubber. It bowed low to the ground while the police stood staring in astonishment. Nelson marched off, pointing his sword at the police. Then the column suddenly sprang back up like a giant catapult, firing the Human Statue onto the top of a nearby building, where he made his getaway.

"Blundering bubblegum!" exclaimed Major Works through the speaker. "He's getting away with the Stone!"

"What stone?" demanded Chuck. "I think it's time you explained what's going on."

There was a pause before the major spoke. "Yes, well, I suppose it is. It's called the Stone of Life, and it was kept inside the orb at the Tower of London. It's an ancient artifact that dates all the way back to the time of the Druids. Legend has it that whoever possesses the Stone can bring anything to life. It is said that's how Stonehenge was created. In the right hands it is a fantastic thing, but in the wrong hands . . ."

"A terrible weapon," said Donnie.

"Exactly," said the major.

"Who else knows about it?" asked Jet.

"It's top secret. I only heard of its

existence when I began working for the Secret Secret Service," said the major.

"It would have been helpful to know about this from the beginning," said Chuck.

"Well, I'm sorry, but here at the Secret Secret Service we take our secrecy very seriously."

"And we take our lives very seriously," said Chuck. "Now, if you don't mind, we'd better get on with our jobs and get that Stone of Life from the Human Statue."

"Very well, but you must stay out of sight!" said Major Works.

"As ninjas trained in the Way of the Scorpion, we know how to shift with the shadows," said Chuck.

"Time for another disguise?" asked Donnie.

"No, but we will need a grappling hook," said Chuck.

"Lucky I always carry a spare, then," replied Donnie.

"Hold on a minute," said Bruce. "There's a pork pie in here with only a couple of bites taken out."

"Bruce," said Chuck. "There is currently a madman terrorizing the streets of London. It's not the time for a snack."

Bruce shoveled the food into his mouth and gulped it down in one. "Ready now."

CHAPTER FOUR

A DUEL WITH JUSTICE

London was in utter chaos. Howling sirens competed with sounds of mass panic. The police had ordered the public to return to their homes and stay inside with the doors locked. Police cars and fire engines filled the streets. In Trafalgar Square, riot police battled to keep the statues at bay. No one noticed the tiny grappling hook fly out of a trash can and attach itself to the top of a church, or the four ninja meerkats quickly scurrying up the line.

From their position on the roof, the

meerkats paused to take in the astonishing scene all around them.

"I just caught a glimpse of the Human Statue heading down the Strand on the surveillance cameras," said Major Works through the speakers on Jet's sunglasses.

"Clan of the Scorpion, let's go catch a statue," said Chuck.

All four of them ran across the church roof, leaping over the street to the next rooftop.

"Look at all those statues," said Jet. "The Human Statue isn't wasting any time."

Strange statues marched along the street below, trampling over anything that got in their way. Armed police shot at them, but the bullets bounced off. The statues barely even registered the attacks.

"Shouldn't we help the police?" asked Bruce.

"We have to get the Stone of Life back," replied Chuck. "That is our mission."

"There's our man now," said Jet, spotting the Human Statue standing on top of a magnificent white building with sloping roofs and splendid towers and turrets.

"Those are the law courts," said Major Works.

On top of the building with the Human Statue were three moving statues. Two of them were gargoyles with hideous misshapen bodies. The other was a woman. She was wearing a long flowing stone dress and held a pair of scales in one hand and a huge sword in the other.

"That's Lady Justice," said Major Works. "Those gargoyles must be from the church."

"This time we need a proper plan of attack," said Chuck.

But Jet wasn't listening. He was bounding over the rooftops toward the Human Statue.

"Human Statue," he shouted. "The name's Flashfeet. Agent Flashfeet. It's time to give yourself up."

"Do you think I'm afraid of a weedy

little rat like you?" he laughed. "I've got justice on my side!"

Lady Justice swung her scales at Jet. He drew his nunchucks and batted them away. She followed up with a sword attack, but Chuck blocked it, clutching his own sword with both paws.

"Justice is swift, ain't she?" said the Human Statue. "Gargoyles, get the other two."

They charged, but Bruce jumped out of danger and the two gargoyles collided with an earth-shattering CRUNCH!

Donnie drew a set of throwing stars from his backpack and hurled them in quick succession, before the gargoyles had time to recover. They would have felled most enemies, but they pinged off the stone gargoyles without causing any harm.

"Agent Flashfeet! Quick! The Human Statue is getting away," said Major Works.

Jet turned and saw that the crook was disappearing over the roofs. Seeing that he was distracted, Justice jabbed her sword at him. Jet performed an astounding double backflip to avoid the attack and narrowly missed falling off the roof.

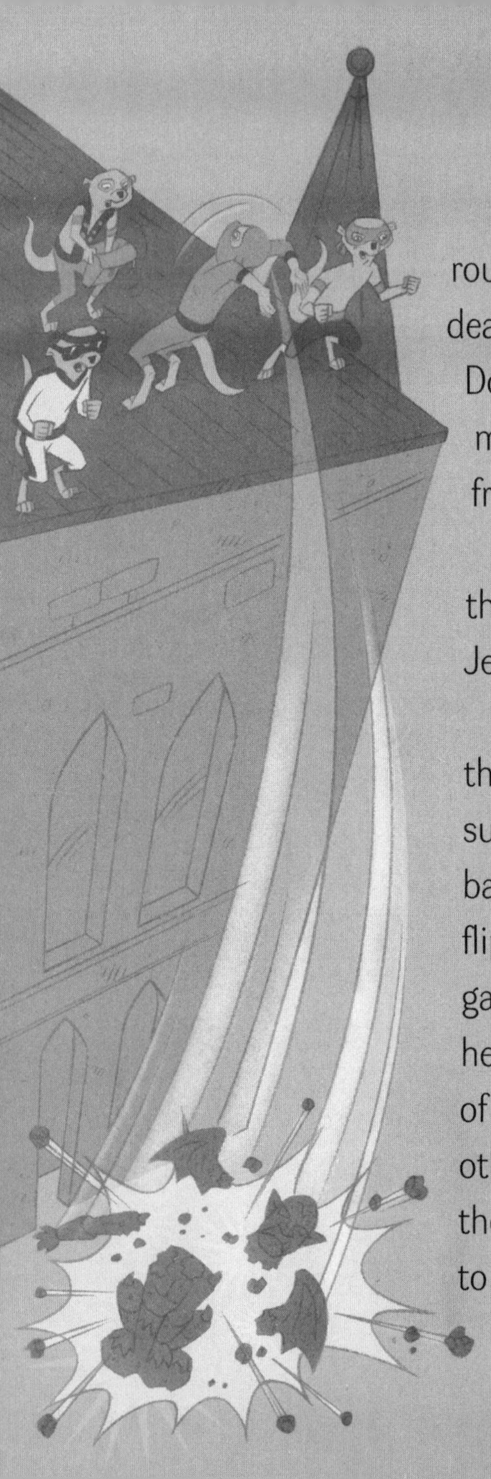

"That's some rough justice she's dealing out," said Donnie, as he pulled missiles and gadgets from his backpack.

"How do we hurt these things?" asked Jet.

"You ground them," replied Bruce, suddenly rolling backward and flipping a surprised gargoyle over his head and off the edge of the building. The others watched as the statue smashed to the ground.

"Now, that's what I call Bruce Force!" said Bruce.

"That's what I call gravitational force," said Donnie.

"That's it, Bruce!" said Jet. "We need to push them off."

"Stop!" said Major Works. "These are valuable statues of great historical interest."

"Historical interest?" said Donnie. "If it hasn't slipped your attention, your historically interesting statues are tearing up the city!"

"They need to be returned to their original positions without damage," insisted the major.

"He's right," said Chuck. "We must use our ninja skills to obtain the Stone of Life without destroying these statues. It's not their fault that they have been brought to life for evil purposes."

Seeing the gargoyle's fate on the pavement, the other statues had begun to climb down the side of the building. Many more were marching through the streets.

"They're all heading the same way," said Jet.

"Let's see where they're going," said Chuck.

He led the others across the roofs, in the same direction as the statues.

"Major Works," said Chuck as they ran. "How many statues are there in London?"

"Somewhere in the region of thirty thousand," replied the major.

"Thirty thousand?" exclaimed Jet. "He can build an army with that many."

"An indestructible army," said Donnie.

"But where are they all going?" asked Bruce.

As the meerkats watched, the statues

turned off the road and entered a red-fronted building with the words "Strand Station" printed in bold letters above the entrance.

"It looks like they're going underground," said Donnie.

CHAPTER FIVE
GOING UNDERGROUND

"We should follow them," said Chuck, as they watched the statues march into the building.

"There's no point in that," said Major Works. "They're trapped. You see, that building isn't an Underground station anymore. It was shut up years ago and no trains go through. I'm going to find out what the police have planned. Agent Flashfeet, keep your team where it is until you hear from me."

"Yes, sir," said Jet.

"*Your* team?" said Donnie and Bruce together.

"I've got the sunglasses," replied Jet defensively.

"Yes, and now it's time to take them off, Jet," said Chuck.

"You're just jealous because he picked me to wear them and be the chief spy," responded Jet.

"We are not spies," said Chuck calmly. "We are the Clan of the Scorpion. We don't follow orders. We follow our instincts. Now tell me, Jet, what are your instincts telling you?"

Jet looked down at the statues and the police cars gathered around the building. Overhead, a helicopter hovered low, keeping an eye on all the winged statues flying into the building.

"I think this has been too carefully

planned to be a mistake," said Jet, removing the sunglasses and placing them on the roof. "We need to find out what's going on, and get the Stone of Life back, not just sit here waiting for instructions!"

Chuck smiled. "Agreed. Donnie, do you have any gray paint?"

"Of course." Donnie pulled two cans of gray spray-paint out of his bag.

"Let's statue up," said Chuck.

"Do me first," said Bruce.

"OK. Keep your eyes shut," said Donnie. He sprayed the two cans at Bruce until he disappeared in a cloud of paint. When it cleared, Bruce was exactly the same color as the statues marching below them.

"Hey Bruce, you feeling OK?" asked Jet.

"Yeah, why?" asked Bruce.

"You seem a bit off color," replied Jet.

Once all four of them looked like statues, they clambered down a drainpipe and across the road, slipping into the line of statues behind an army sergeant and two Queen Victorias. A horse with wings sat on top of the building, looking out for any signs of an aerial assault from the police. It didn't see the meerkats march by, right under its nose. Inside, they saw that the statues had bashed a hole in a wall to

reveal a huge spiral staircase heading underground.

"Where do you think we're going?" asked Bruce.

"Keep your voice down," said Chuck. "We must remain undercover."

At the bottom of the stairs was a train platform where the statues were silently gathering, like an extremely odd assortment of commuters on their way to work. The meerkats darted between the legs of the statues, looking for the Human Statue.

"It must be the old tube station platform," whispered Chuck.

"They'll be waiting a while for a train then," said Bruce.

"I'm not sure about that," said Donnie.

A rumbling sound filled the tunnel, followed by a cold gust of wind. Through the mass of legs, the meerkats saw a train pull into the platform. The statues piled into the empty cars and the meerkats were whisked along with them. As they reached the door, Chuck directed them up the back of a stone bear and onto the top of the subway train.

"What's going on?" asked Bruce.

"The Human Statue is fooling the police, keeping them focused on this building, while moving his army elsewhere," said Jet.

The doors closed and the train began to move, quickly picking up speed. It rattled through the tunnel at a fantastic rate and

the meerkats had to cling on tight to prevent themselves from being thrown off. Eventually the train slowed down and pulled into another abandoned platform. It stopped and the doors slid open. At once the statues began to march off the train.

The meerkats peered over the top.

"Any idea where we are, Donnie?" asked Chuck.

Donnie pulled out his phone and clicked on the GPS function. "I can't get a signal."

All of a sudden, the meerkats felt a stony hand grab them and they were pulled from their hiding place by Charlie Chaplin.

"I didn't think I'd brought any rodent statues to life," said the Human Statue, suddenly appearing behind Chaplin, with Lord Nelson by his side.

"We're not rodents," said Jet. "We're meerkats."

"Whatever," said the Human Statue dismissively. He was holding a stone. It looked just like an ordinary pebble but it had to be the Stone of Life.

"What are you up to?" asked Chuck.

"I'm Stan Still and my statue army is going to bring this city to a *standstill*. No longer will people pass me by without even noticing. Finally, they will pay attention to me! Soon every statue in this city will be under my control—I will leave no stone unturned!"

"Oh, great," said Donnie. "Another pun-obsessed super villain."

"Shut it, you flea-ridden rat," snapped the Human Statue. "Nelson, take this mouthy meerkat and make sure he can't escape. Chaplin, hold on to the others. You're taking them on the last train out of here." He pulled out a small electronic device. "This remote control operates the train, you see. I designed it myself."

"No matter where you send us, we'll still find you," said Jet.

"I don't think so," said the Human Statue. "You see, I don't need this train anymore. I'm sending you on a crash collision with the end of the tunnel." He chuckled.

"Tell me one thing," said Chuck. "How did you learn about the Stone of Life?"

"I got a tip-off, as it happens," he replied. "Now, it's time for you lot to go to your final destination."

The two statues stepped onto the subway with the meerkats firmly in their grip. The doors slid shut and the train started to move.

THE SUBWAY OF DEATH

The meerkats tried to wriggle free, but the statues held them tightly as the train went faster and faster.

"We need to get off before the train crashes," said Donnie.

"If I could get free, I'd use some Bruce Force," said Bruce.

"And I'd Ninja-boom my way out," said Jet, struggling.

But it was no use—the statues' hold was rock solid.

"Any ideas, Donnie?" asked Chuck.

"Loads," said Donnie. "Only they all involve not being in the vice-like grip of this statue's hand. Nelson is squeezing me so hard that if he's not careful he'll set off one of my gadgets. Hold on—I've got it!" He wriggled around.

"What's 'it'?" asked Bruce.

"You'll see. I'm just making sure I've got the right angle," said Donnie. "There. Now I need to make him angry."

"You want to make him angry?!" exclaimed Chuck.

"How do you even make a statue angry?" asked Bruce.

"I know," said Jet. "Hey, statues, do you know what the pigeons call you?" He sniggered. "Target practice!"

"How does it feel to be a bird-poop bull's-eye, Nelson?" said Donnie.

Nelson looked down at Donnie and squeezed hard, trying to crush him. As he did so, his huge thumb pushed one of the buttons on Donnie's backpack. A grappling hook shot out, latched on to a red lever by the train door and yanked it down. Above the lever were the words "Emergency Stop."

There was a screeching sound as the brakes went on but the train was traveling too fast to come to a standstill. It jolted violently and the statues crashed to the ground, releasing the meerkats as they fell. They ran to the end of the passenger car and, with a cry of "Bruce Force!", Bruce kicked off the back door.

"Mind the gap!" yelled Jet as they all leaped out. The meerkats landed in forward rolls, just as the train hit the end of the tunnel.

"Take cover!" cried Chuck, shielding his eyes from the explosion.

"That was close," said Bruce.

As the dust settled in the gloomy tunnel, they heard another rumbling sound.

"Sounds like thunder," said Jet.

"You don't get thunder underground," said Donnie. "The tunnel is collapsing!"

"Quickly, this way!" ordered Chuck.

The meerkats ran as fast as they could down one of the tunnels as large chunks of rock fell from the ceiling.

Eventually, they reached another station and climbed up onto the deserted platform.

"Everyone ready to continue our mission and retrieve the Stone of Life?" asked Chuck, wiping the dust from his sleeves.

"You mean ready to go and fight an army made up of several tons of solid stone and metal that massively outnumbers us?" said Jet.

"Yes," said Chuck.

"You bet we're ready," said Jet.

"Bring it on!" said Bruce.

"Let's rock!" said Donnie.

CHAPTER SEVEN
THE LONDON EYE

A staircase led up from the subway station to the surface, where it looked like a secret cover had been pushed away in the corner of a small park by the river. It had grown dark while they'd been underground and a few stars shone in the night sky above. At one end of the park was a huge wheel with slowly revolving observation pods, known as the London Eye. In front of it was the army of statues. On the other side of the river they could see helicopters circling the Strand Station building.

"You were right, Chuck," whispered Donnie. "While the police are watching the underground station across the river, the army has gathered here unnoticed, so they'll have the advantage of surprise when they attack."

"I bet he's left a few statues over there to give the impression they're all inside," said Chuck. "It's down to us to get hold of the Stone of Life and stop this madness."

"There he is now," said Jet.

The Human Statue climbed up onto a platform in front of the London Eye and addressed his army, but the meerkats were too far back to hear him. They slipped into the crowd, moving swiftly and silently among the forest of feet. As they got nearer, they could finally hear what the Human Statue was saying.

"Statues of London, we've been ignored and unnoticed for too long now. Finally you'll rise up and take this city. Every last one of you will be brought to life and then we'll rule the world!"

The Human Statue held up the Stone of Life and the statues raised their arms in a solemn, silent salute. But from the darkness came the sound of someone clapping slowly. The Human Statue turned around to see who it was. A shadowy figure in a tall hat stepped out of the darkness.

"The Ringmaster!" gasped all four meerkats as one.

By the Ringmaster's side were the clowns, Grimsby and Sheffield, and Herr Flick, holding a knife in each hand. At his feet was Doris the Dancing Dog.

"What a moving speech, Mr. Still," said the Ringmaster.

"Who are you?" asked the Human Statue.

"They call me the Ringmaster," he replied. "You've done an excellent job here, but now I'll have to relieve you of the Stone of Life."

"No way," began the Human Statue, but before he knew what was happening, Grimsby pulled out a custard pie and hurled it at his face. Then Sheffield tripped him up with his huge feet and Doris pirouetted, spun in midair, and snatched the Stone from his hands. The Ringmaster took it from her mouth.

"Good dog," said the Ringmaster. "Now the statues of London will listen to *me*."

"I wouldn't try telling them any jokes," said Grimsby.

"Why?" asked Sheffield.

"Because they seem a bit stone-faced."

The two clowns laughed heartily and grabbed the Human Statue, gripping his arms tightly to stop him from escaping.

"Quiet, you two," said the Ringmaster. "Statues of London," he cried. "Listen to your new master. I believe we may have some unwelcome guests. Stamp your feet, use your weapons. Let's flush them out."

Suddenly, every set of feet started stamping and sharp swords of stone and metal shot up and down, prodding the ground. The meerkats had no choice but to move quickly into the open, right in front of the Ringmaster.

"Ah, the Clan of the Scorpion. How nice to see you! You've fallen right into my trap."

"Your trap?" said Chuck. "We are here to take back the Stone of Life."

"Yes, but only because I wanted you here," he replied. "You see, I captured each and every one of Major Works's spies, knowing he would have no choice but to contact his old friend Grandmaster One-Eye for help. The British Secret Secret Service is no secret to me. Since capturing his spies, I have been watching your every move through Major Works's surveillance system. His equipment is not as sophisticated as he thinks."

The Ringmaster held the Stone of Life aloft and the statues formed a wall around the meerkats.

"And now there is no way that you can escape," he said.

"But how did you know the Human Statue was going to steal the Stone?" asked Donnie.

"Because I was the one who tipped him off about the Stone in order to lure you into this trap."

"You used me!" said the Human Statue.

"Yes," said the Ringmaster. "This army has only one purpose. They will finally rid me of the Clan of the Scorpion. I will take the Stone and begin my world domination campaign elsewhere. Statues, I order you to destroy the Clan of the Scorpion!"

"Why, you rotten circus freak . . ." The Human Statue wriggled free from the clowns' grip and ran at the Ringmaster. For a moment the two men wrestled, then Doris bit the Human Statue's ankle, making him cry out in pain and fall to the ground. Quick as a flash, Herr Flick released a series of knives, pinning him to the ground by his clothes.

The Ringmaster held up the Stone of Life. “Circus troupe, let’s go to the boat,” he said. “Good-bye, meerkats.”

CHAPTER EIGHT

THE QUAKE MAKER

As the statues attacked from every side, Chuck drew his sword, spun around, and announced, "Before the Clan, each enemy cowers, for now we fight till victory is ours!"

The statues with wings flew over the top and swooped down at the meerkats. Those with weapons thrust, lunged, and swung, and the statues with sharp teeth snapped their jaws. Jet dodged an attack from a soldier, rolled under his legs, leaped up, and kicked his back. The stone soldier staggered forward, knocking over a row of statues, who clattered to the ground in confusion.

A lion lunged at Bruce, but he was too quick. The lion lowered his head to attack again but Bruce ran onto his back and jumped away before the lion had time to turn around.

Chuck found himself up against Lady Justice again. He was bravely fighting her

off, blocking one attack, then spinning around to block another, moving at incredible speed. Lady Justice took a swing at him, which he avoided by leaping onto her scales. She tried to get him off by swinging them viciously, but Chuck rolled backward and watched as the scales collided with Queen Victoria's head, sending her reeling.

"That's what I call tipping the scales in your favor," said Donnie, who was using a slingshot to fend off an eagle and a dragon.

But no matter how many statues the meerkats dodged, there were more behind, waiting to attack.

"We need to get the Stone of Life!" said Chuck.

"I'm on it," said Donnie. He pulled a tag on the side of his backpack, igniting two jets at the bottom, which propelled him up in the air. He pulled the toggles to steer and flew down toward the river, but was closely pursued by two vicious owls.

"Donnie's got a tail," cried Chuck.

"So? We've all got tails," said Bruce.

"I mean those owls are following him. He needs help!"

"No problem," said Bruce, ducking a ball and chain swung by a Roman gladiator.

Bruce grabbed the ball and, with a loud grunt, yanked it out of the gladiator's hand. He then lobbed it up at one of the owls, hitting his target and sending it colliding with the other.

"Nice one, Bruce," yelled Donnie. "Two birds with one stone!"

Donnie could see that the Ringmaster and Doris had already climbed into the boat. Grimsby and Sheffield were still on the jetty, untying the tethered rope.

Just as they released the boat, he swooped down and barged into them, sending the two clowns into the water with a huge SPLASH!

"Hey, boss, give us a ring, would you?" shouted Grimsby.

"What good will a phone call be?" said Sheffield, flailing about in the water.

"I mean a rubber ring," said Grimsby.

"Come on, you two idiots," said the Ringmaster, throwing a couple of rubber rings for the clowns and pulling them back toward the boat.

Donnie made to fly after them, but felt

something holding him back. He turned his head to see a stone dragon gripping his backpack in its mouth. He slipped his arms out of the straps and dropped to the ground in time to see his backpack being torn to bits by the dragon's rock-hard teeth.

"Do you know how much stuff was in that, you dumb dragon?" demanded Donnie.

The dragon landed and bared its teeth at Donnie, preparing to attack. At that moment, the ground began to shake and Donnie watched as the dragon lost its footing and toppled into the river.

"Whoa! What's happening?" cried Donnie. He ran back up the jetty to see that the entire army of statues had fallen over. In among them was Jet, standing with his legs apart.

"Ninja-boom-boom, shake the room," he said. "That's what I call a Quake Maker."

Chuck and Bruce were standing over the Human Statue, who was still pinned to the ground by Herr Flick's knives.

"Set me free!" he cried. "I'll give you the Stone of Life!"

"What?" said Donnie. "But the Ringmaster's got the Stone."

"Oh no, he hasn't," said the Human Statue. "It's in my pocket. I swapped it for an ordinary stone when I attacked him."

Chuck reached into the Human Statue's pocket and pulled out a stone.

"How do we know this isn't just an ordinary stone?" asked Donnie. "Why should we believe you?"

"Just try it," said the Human Statue. "Then you'll see that I'm telling the truth. Now set me free!"

"No chance," said Bruce. "The police will deal with you."

"Statues of London," shouted Chuck, holding the Stone of Life aloft. "It's now time to return to your plinths and to your natural state."

The statues got up obediently and began to make their way out of the park, leaving the meerkats guarding the Human Statue. They were just discussing their next move when Major Works appeared.

"Stammering statues!" he exclaimed. "Excellent work, meerkats. The Clan of the Scorpion is a team to be reckoned with. I've been observing your movements on the surveillance cameras. It took a while to find you after you disobeyed my orders."

“Ninjas do not follow orders. We get the job done,” said Chuck. “If you want someone to take orders, I suggest you get a waiter.”

“I wouldn’t mind being a waiter,” said Bruce. “As long as I got to eat all the leftovers.”

“Here is the Stone of Life,” said Chuck, handing the Stone to Major Works. “Our original mission was to recover the orb, which we have not done. But I think this man will be able to help you with that.”

“Ah, the Human Statue,” said Major Works. “The police will be delighted to have him back behind bars.”

The major looked down at the pitiful figure of the Human Statue, struggling helplessly to free himself. He turned back to the meerkats. “Thank you, Clan of the Scorpion—your assistance on this mission has been very impressive. Would you consider continuing your work for the Secret Secret Service? You'd make excellent spies—especially you, Agent Flashfeet."

"Thanks," said Jet, "but I think I'm a better ninja than spy."

"We couldn't stay here," said Chuck. "The Ringmaster is still at large. We must continue in our efforts to stop his plans for world domination."

"Very well," said Major Works. "I'll arrange for a special spy plane to fly you back to your base."

"You mean we don't have to hide in the luggage compartment?" said Bruce.

"That's right," said Major Works. "Our spy planes have the latest films and top-notch catering."

"Movies? Food?" exclaimed Bruce. "Can't we become spies after all?"

"Maybe we could pop back and work for the major over the Christmas holidays," suggested Donnie.

"Christmas? Why Christmas?" asked Major Works.

"Then we could be mince spies," Donnie chuckled.

GOFISH

QUESTIONS FOR THE AUTHOR

Gareth P. Jones

What did you want to be when you grew up?
At various points, a writer, a musician, an intergalactic bounty hunter and, for a limited period, a graphic designer. (I didn't know what that meant, but I liked the way it sounded.)

When did you realize you wanted to be a writer?
I don't remember realizing it. I have always loved stories. From a very young age, I enjoyed making them up. As I'm not very good at making things up on the spot, this invariably involved having to write them down.

What's an embarrassing childhood memory?
Seriously? There are too many. I have spent my entire life saying and doing embarrassing things. Just thinking about some of them is making me cringe. Luckily, I have a terrible memory, so I can't remember them all, but no, I'm not going to write any down for you. If I did that, I'd never be able to forget them.

What's your favorite childhood memory?

To be honest with you, I don't remember my childhood very well at all (I told you I had a bad memory), but I do recall how my dad used to tell me stories. He would make them up as he went along, most likely borrowing all sorts of elements from the books he was reading without me knowing.

As a young person, who did you look up to most?

My mom and dad, Prince, Michael Jackson, all of Monty Python, and Stephen Fry.

What was your favorite thing about school?

Laughing with my friends.

What was your least favorite thing about school?

I had a bit of a hard time when I moved from the Midlands to London at the age of twelve because I had a funny accent. But don't worry, it was all right in the end.

What were your hobbies as a kid? What are your hobbies now?

I love listening to and making music. My hobbies haven't really changed over the years, except that there's a longer list of instruments now. When I get a chance, I like idling away the day playing trumpet, guitar, banjo, ukulele, mandolin (and piano if there's one in the vicinity). I also like playing out with my friends.

What was your first job, and what was your "worst" job?

My first job was working as a waiter. That's probably my worst job, too. As my dad says, I was a remarkably grumpy waiter. I'm not big on all that serving-people malarkey.

What book is on your nightstand now?

I have a pile of books from my new publisher. I'm trying to get through them before I meet the authors. I'm half-way through *Maggot Moon* by Sally Gardner, which is written in the amazing voice of a dyslexic boy.

How did you celebrate publishing your first book?

The first time I saw one of my books in a shop, I was so excited that I caused something of a commotion. I managed to persuade an unsuspecting customer to buy it so I could sign it for her son.

Where do you write your books?

Anywhere and everywhere. Here are some of the locations I have written the Ninja Meerkats series: On the 185 and the 176 buses in London, various airplanes, Hong Kong, Melbourne, all over New Zealand, a number of cafes and bars between San Diego and San Francisco, New Quay in South Wales, and my kitchen.

What sparked your imagination for the Ninja Meerkats?

The idea came from the publishing house, but from the moment I heard it, I really wanted to write it. It reminded me of lots of action-packed cartoons I used to watch when I was young. I love the fact that I get to cram in lots of jokes and puns, fast action, and crazy outlandish plots.

The Ninja Meerkats are awesome fighters; have you ever studied martial arts? If so, what types?
Ha, no. If I was to get into a fight, my tactic would be to fall over and hope that whoever was attacking me lost interest.

If you were a Ninja Meerkat, what would your name be?
Hmm, how about Gareth *POW!* Jones?

What's your favorite exhibit or animal at the zoo?
Funnily enough, I like the meerkats. I was at a zoo watching them the other day when it started to rain. They suddenly ran for cover, looking exactly like their human visitors.

What's Bruce's favorite food?
Anything with the words ALL YOU CAN EAT written above it.

If you had a catchphrase like Bruce Force! or Ninja-Boom! what would it be?
That's a tricky one. How about PEN POWER!

If you were a Ninja Meerkat, what would your special ninja skill be?
I like to think I'd be like Jet, and always working on a new skill. When I got into school, I took the Random Move

Generator! We used it to come up with new moves, like the Floating Butterfly Punch and the Ultimate Lemon Punch.

What is your favorite thing about real-life meerkats? Have you ever met a meerkat?
I was lucky enough to go into a meerkat enclosure recently. They were crawling all over me, trying to get a good view. It was brilliant.

What challenges do you face in the writing process, and how do you overcome them?
The challenge with writing the Ninja Meerkats books is mostly about the plotting. It's trying to get all the twists and turns to work, and to avoid them feeling predictable. When I hit problems, I write down as many options as I can think of from the completely ordinary to utterly ridiculous. Once they're all down on paper, the right answer normally jumps out at me.

Which of your characters is most like you?
I'd like to say that I'm wise and noble like Chuck, but I'm probably more like the Ringmaster as we're both always coming up with new ways to take over the world.

What makes you laugh out loud?
My friends.

What do you do on a rainy day?
Play guitar, write, watch TV, or go out with my sword-handled umbrella.

What's your idea of fun?

Answering questionnaires about myself. Actually, tomorrow, I'm going to a music festival with my wife where we will dance and cavort. That should be fun.

What's your favorite song?

There are far too many to mention, but today I think I'll go for "Feel Good Inc." by Gorillaz.

Who is your favorite fictional character?

Another tricky one, but today I'll say Ged from the Earthsea Trilogy by Ursula K. Le Guin.

What was your favorite book when you were a kid?

As a child, I especially loved *The Phantom Tollbooth* by Norton Juster.

What's your favorite TV show or movie?

Raiders of the Lost Ark.

If you were stranded on a desert island, who would you want for company?

My wife and son, then probably my friend Pete, as he's really handy and would be able to make and build things.

If you could travel anywhere in the world, where would you go and what would you do?

I'd like to go to Canada next. Ideally, I'd like to go and live there for a bit. I've never been to South America. There are also lots of parts of America I haven't visited yet.

If you could travel in time, where would you go and what would you do?
I think I'd travel to the future and see what's changed and whether anyone's invented a new kind of umbrella.

What's the best advice you have ever received about writing?
Don't tell the story, show the story.

What advice do you wish someone had given you when you were younger?
Everything's probably going to be fine, so it's best to enjoy yourself.

Do you ever get writer's block? What do you do to get back on track?
It feels like tempting fate, but I don't really believe in writer's block. I think if you can't write, you're doing the wrong thing. You may need to plan or jot down options or go for a walk.

What do you want readers to remember about your books?
I'd settle for a general feeling of having enjoyed them.

What would you do if you ever stopped writing?
I'd do a full stop. If this is for an American audience, I guess that would be a period.

What should people know about you?
I'm a very silly man.

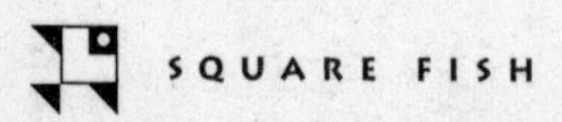

What do you like best about yourself?
I'm a very silly man.

Do you have any strange or funny habits? Did you when you were a kid?
I talk to myself a lot, which is probably pretty common, but the difference is that I don't listen to what I'm saying.

Danger erupts on Dragon Island when the Ringmaster discovers the volcanic island's precious secret. Can the meerkats stop his evil plan?

It's time for the Ninja Meerkats to leap into action!

Ninja-Boom!

Two fishermen stood on the beach, watching the row boat make its way out to sea.

"Where do you think it's going?" asked one of the men.

"Looks like it's heading for Dragon Island," replied the other, pointing to an ominous-looking island with a huge volcano at its center sending out red smoke into the sky.

"My cousin told me the island's name is because of the dragon smoke that billows from its center," said the first fisherman.

"Your cousin is a superstitious fool," said the other. "The smoke comes from the volcano."

"So why does it turn red every five years?"

"No one knows. I even swam to the island as a boy to try to find out, but there's nothing there other than wild lemurs."

Had the two fishermen seen the boat up close, they would have realized that the rower was a shop dummy, disguised as a fisherman. It was being operated by a remote control held by one of four ninja meerkats onboard.

"Another brilliant disguise, Donnie," said Chuck.

"Thanks," replied Donnie. "I call it the M.O.R.B.—Mannequin Operated Rowing Boat."

"Why do we need a disguise anyway?" asked Bruce.

"The invitation said we should arrive in secret," replied Chuck.

"The invitation for me to be crowned the Ultimate Dragon Warrior," added Jet. "Ninja-boom!" He leaped up and punched the air.

"Jet," shouted Donnie. "You're rocking—"

"You're right," Jet interrupted. "Being invited to compete in the most awesome kung-fu contest in the world *is* rocking, isn't it?"

"I mean, you're rocking the boat," said Donnie. "Besides, the invitation was for all

of us. Any one of us could win."

"Ha! It's bound to be me," said Jet.

"Jet, boasting is not a good thing," said Chuck.

"Yeah, my uncle almost died when it happened to him," said Bruce.

"He died from boasting?" asked Donnie.

"Yep," said Bruce. "It turned out he was allergic."

"I believe that was a bee sting, Bruce," said Chuck. "And actually, it could be that *none* of us takes home the title. Remember, the invitation said there would be eight competitors in total."

"I'll scare off the competition with my Super-charged Shock Attack!" said Jet.

"What's that?" asked Bruce.

"It's my new move," explained Jet. "You rub your feet on the ground and charge yourself up with static electricity, then use

it to shock your opponent."

Donnie smirked. "If you want to shock them, just tell them how long you spent looking in the mirror this morning."

As the boat got closer to the island, the red smoke from the volcano blocked out the sun and threw the boat into the shadow of the island.

"Donnie, what did your background check reveal about this island?" asked Chuck.

"Very little," replied Donnie. "It's named Dragon Island because of the red smoke, but everything else is a mystery."

"Ooh, spooky," said Bruce.

"Are we sure this isn't one of the Ringmaster's traps?" asked Chuck. "A strange invitation, a remote island—I wouldn't put it past him."

"No way," said Jet. "The Trials of Dragon Island are legendary. Once every five years, when the volcano smoke turns red, the world's finest martial-arts fighters are summoned to compete for the title of Ultimate Dragon Warrior."